Alice's adventures begin as she lies on a grassy bank one sunny afternoon. After following the White Rabbit down a rabbit hole she meets all kinds of strange and wonderful characters. She talks with the Cheshire Cat, swims with the Mouse, takes tea with the Mad Hatter and plays croquet with the Queen.

Lewis Carroll's original Alice's Adventures in Wonderland *was written over one hundred years ago. In this version the story is delightfully retold and beautifully illustrated for young readers.*

Please note that although many of Lewis Carroll's original characters appear in this version of Alice in Wonderland it has not been possible to include them all.

British Library Cataloguing in Publication Data

Collins, Joan, *1917-*
    Alice in Wonderland. — (Ladybird children's classics)
    I. Title   II. Boon-Jenkins, Debbie   III. Carroll, Lewis
    823'.914[J]   PZ7
    ISBN 0-7214-0967-9

First edition

Published by Ladybird Books Ltd Loughborough Leicestershire UK
Ladybird Books Inc Lewiston Maine 04240 USA

ALICE IN WONDERLAND

by Lewis Carroll

retold by Joan Collins
illustrated by Debbie Boon-Jenkins

Ladybird Books

Down the rabbit hole

Alice was tired of sitting by her sister on the grassy bank, and having nothing to do. Her sister was reading a book with no pictures or conversations in it. It looked very dull.

It was a hot day and Alice was feeling sleepy. She was wondering whether to get up and make a daisy chain, when suddenly a white rabbit with pink eyes ran close by her.

'Oh, dear! Oh, dear! I shall be late!' the White Rabbit said. It took a watch out of its waistcoat pocket, looked at it, and hurried on. Alice had

never seen a rabbit with a waistcoat pocket
before, nor one with a watch to take out of it.
She jumped to her feet and ran after it, just in
time to see it pop down a large rabbit hole under
the hedge. Down went Alice after it, never
thinking how she was going to get out again.

The rabbit hole went on like a tunnel for
some way and then it
dipped suddenly.

Alice found herself falling down a very deep well. She was falling slowly so she had time to look around and see all sorts of interesting things on shelves and in cupboards on the way.

'I wonder how many thousand miles I've fallen?' she thought. 'I must be somewhere near the centre of the earth. Perhaps I'll fall right through to the other side!'

But just then, *thump*, *thump*, *thump*, down she came, on a heap of leaves, without hurting herself at all. Ahead of her, at the end of a long passage, she saw the White Rabbit hurrying along. 'Oh, my ears and whiskers! How late it's getting!' she heard it say, as it turned the corner.

6

The gold key

When Alice reached the corner, the White Rabbit had gone. She found herself in a long hall, lighted by lamps in the ceiling. There were doors all the way round, but they were locked. How was she going to get out?

Then she saw a little three-legged table, made of glass. On top of it was a gold key. But it was too small to unlock any of the doors. Then Alice noticed a low curtain. Behind it she found a tiny door, only fifteen inches high. The key fitted it perfectly!

Alice had to kneel down to look through the door. There was a small passage that led to the loveliest garden you ever saw. But Alice was too big even to get her head through the doorway. 'I wish I could shut up like a telescope!' she said to herself.

She walked back to the glass table. To her surprise there was a bottle on it, which had not been there before. A label round its neck said DRINK ME in large letters. Alice took a sip. It was delicious and tasted of all Alice's favourite foods. So she drank it up.

'What a curious feeling!' said Alice. 'I *must* be shutting up like a telescope!' And so she was! Soon she was only ten inches high, just the size to go through the little door into the lovely garden.

Poor Alice! She had left the gold key on top of the glass table. Now she was too small to reach it. She tried to climb up the slippery glass table leg, until she was tired out, and sat down and cried.

Then she
noticed a
little glass
box on the
floor. Inside it
was a cake, with
EAT ME marked
on it in currants.
'Perhaps it will
make me grow,'
thought Alice. She
nibbled it till she had
finished it all up.

The pool of tears

'Curiouser and
curiouser!' cried
Alice. 'Now I'm
opening out like the
largest telescope in
the world!'

Her feet were so
far away that she
wondered how she
would get her shoes
and stockings off
and on. Then her
head struck against
the ceiling. Alice
was more than nine
feet high!

She picked up the little gold key and hurried off to the garden door. But poor Alice could only look into the garden with one eye, by lying down on the floor. She sat down and began to cry again. 'What a great baby you are!' she scolded herself but she could not stop crying. Soon there was a large pool of tears around her, reaching halfway down the hall.

The White Rabbit returns

There was a pattering of feet in the distance. Alice dried her eyes and saw the White Rabbit once again. He was carrying a fan and a pair of white gloves, and muttering, 'Oh, the Duchess! Oh, the Duchess! Won't she be cross if I've kept her waiting!'

'Please, sir, could you help me?' said Alice, timidly. But when he saw her, he dropped his fan and gloves, and scurried off as fast as he could. Alice picked up the things he had dropped. It was very hot so she began to fan herself. She felt very strange.

'I'm not at all my usual self!' she thought. 'Perhaps I've changed into somebody else! I'll see if I still know the things I learned at school:

four times five is twelve, and five times six is thirteen...' she said. 'London is the capital of Paris, and Paris is the capital of Rome... That can't be right! I *must* be somebody else!' she sobbed.

Then she noticed that she had managed to put on one of the White Rabbit's little gloves. 'I'm small again!' she cried, and ran off to the garden door. But now it was shut and the gold key was back on the glass table.

'Now things are worse than ever!' Her foot slipped, and *splash*! she was up to her chin in salt water, in the pool of tears.

The Mouse's tale

Alice soon found that she was not alone: a Mouse was swimming a little way off. To Alice it looked as big as a hippopotamus.

'Oh, Mouse!' she said, politely. 'Do you know the way out of this pool?' The Mouse did not answer.

'Perhaps it's a French mouse,' Alice thought, 'and doesn't speak English.' She only knew one

sentence in French, from school. 'Où est mon chat?' she asked, hopefully. The Mouse nearly jumped out of the water and quivered with fright.

'Oh, I beg your pardon!' apologised Alice. 'I forgot mice don't like cats!'

'Would *you* like cats – or dogs – if you were me?' squeaked the Mouse indignantly.

'I suppose not!' said Alice, and they swam together to the shore.

13

A strange collection of birds and animals had gathered there. They were running races to get themselves dry, and Alice and the Mouse joined in. When the Mouse had got his breath back, he began to tell Alice why he hated '**C** and **D**', looking around nervously in case any cats and dogs were about.

'Mine is a long and sad tale,' he said.

Alice was looking at his tail as he spoke.

'It *is* long,' she said, 'but why do you call it *sad*?' So when he began his story, Alice's idea of it was something like this:

'Fury said to a
mouse, That
he met in the
house, ''Let
us both go
to law: *I* will
prosecute
you. Come,
I'll take no
denial, we
must have the
trial, for
really this
morning I've
nothing
to do.''
Said the
mouse to the
cur, ''Such
a trial,
dear Sir,
With
no jury
or judge,
would be
wasting
our
breath.''
''I'll be
judge, I'll
be jury,''
said
cunning
old Fury:
''I'll
try the
whole
cause
and
condemn
you
to
death.'' '

15

'You're not attending,' said the Mouse crossly.

'Yes, I am! I think you'd got to the fifth bend,' said Alice.

'I had NOT!' said the Mouse sharply.

'A knot?' said Alice, always ready to help. 'Let me undo it!' But the Mouse was offended and would not stay to finish his story.

Advice from a caterpillar

Meanwhile the White Rabbit's fan and gloves had vanished, so had the pool of tears, the hall and the glass table. Instead Alice found herself on the edge of a wood.

She ran through grass and flowers till she came to a mushroom which was as big as she was. On top of it sat a large blue caterpillar, with its arms folded, quietly smoking a hookah. (A hookah is a sort of long curly Turkish pipe.) The Caterpillar took no notice of her.

After a while, it took the hookah out of its mouth and asked in a sleepy voice, 'Who are *you*?'

Poor Alice was not at all sure who she was. 'I can't remember things as I used to and I don't stay the same size for ten minutes together!' she said.

'What size do you want to be?' asked the Caterpillar.

'A little larger than I am now! Three inches is such a silly size to be!'

The Caterpillar drew itself up to its full height. It was exactly three inches tall! Then it began to crawl away.

'One side will make you taller, one side shorter,' it remarked.

'One side of what?' asked Alice.

'Of the mushroom, of course!' said the Caterpillar crossly, as it crawled out of sight.

Alice put her arms round the edges of the mushroom, as far as she could reach, and broke off two pieces. She nibbled each piece in turn till she had managed to bring her height up to just nine inches. Then she set off again till she came to a house.

Alice went up to the door and knocked timidly. There was a most extraordinary noise going on inside – howling, sneezing, and every so often a crash, as if a dish had been broken. There was no answer so she pushed the door open and marched in.

Pig and pepper

The door led into a large kitchen full of smoke.
The Duchess was sitting on a three-legged stool
in the middle, nursing a baby. The cook was
leaning over the fire, stirring an iron
pan full of soup and shaking a
pepper-pot into it.

The air was thick with
pepper. The Duchess was
sneezing, and the baby was
howling and sneezing in
turns. Only the cook was
not sneezing. Neither
was a large cat, which
was lying on the
hearthrug, grinning from
ear to ear.

'Why does your cat grin
like that?' asked Alice.

'It's a Cheshire Cat!'
said the Duchess. 'PIG!'

Alice was startled.
She thought that the
Duchess was addressing
her, but it was the
baby she meant. Then
the cook took the pan
off the fire and began
throwing the soup over
everything within reach.

When it was all gone, she threw the poker and tongs, saucepans, dishes and plates at the Duchess and the baby.

'Oh, please mind what you're doing!' cried Alice, as a large saucepan lid whizzed past the baby's nose.

The Duchess took no notice, but began to sing a lullaby to the baby. She threw it up and down as she sang, and gave it a violent shake at the end of each line.

'Speak roughly to your little boy,
  And beat him when he sneezes:
He only does it to annoy,
  Because he knows it teases.'

CHORUS
(in which the cook and the baby joined in)
'Wow! Wow! Wow!'

'Here! You may nurse it for a bit, if you like,' the Duchess said to Alice, flinging the baby at her as she spoke. 'I must go and get ready to play croquet with the Queen.'

Alice could hardly hold the baby, it wriggled so. She carried it out into the open air and looked into its face. It had a very turned-up nose and its eyes were very small. Suddenly it grunted. Alice looked at it in alarm. It had turned into a *PIG!*

She put it down quickly and it trotted happily away into the wood. 'If it had grown up, it would have been a ugly child!' thought Alice. 'But it makes quite a handsome pig.'

The Cheshire Cat

Next moment, she was surprised to see the Cheshire Cat sitting and grinning at her on the branch of a tree.

'Do any other people live near here?' asked Alice.

'In *that* direction,' said the Cat, waving its right paw, 'lives a Hatter. And in *that* direction,' waving its other paw, 'lives a March Hare. Visit either: they're both mad. We're all mad here. I'm mad. You're mad.'

'How do you know *I'm* mad?' said Alice, indignantly.

'You must be,' said the Cat, 'or you wouldn't have come here. Are you going to play croquet with the Queen today?'

'I haven't been invited yet,' said Alice.

'You'll see *me* there!' said the Cat, and vanished.

While Alice was still looking at the place where it had been, it suddenly appeared again.

'What became of the baby? I forgot to ask,' it said.

'It turned into a pig,' said Alice. 'I wish you wouldn't disappear so quickly! It makes me giddy!'

'All right,' said the Cat. And this time it vanished quite slowly, beginning with the end of its tail, and ending with its grin, which remained for some time after the rest of it had gone.

'Well, I've often seen a cat without a grin,' said Alice. 'But I've never seen a grin without a cat before!'

The Mad Hatter's tea party

Alice easily recognised the March Hare's house when she came to it. The chimneys were shaped like ears and the roof was covered with fur.

At a table in front of the house, the March Hare and the Hatter were having tea. The Dormouse was sitting between them. It was asleep, and the other two were using it as a cushion, resting their elbows on it, and talking over its head. The table was a large one, but the three were all crowded into one corner.

'No room! No room!' they cried out when they saw Alice coming.

'There's plenty of room!' said Alice indignantly, sitting down in a large armchair.

'Have some wine!' said the March Hare.

'I don't see any,' said Alice, looking round.

'There isn't any!' said the March Hare.

'It wasn't very polite of you to offer it, then!' said Alice, angrily.

'It wasn't very polite of *you* to sit down without being asked!' replied the March Hare.

Then the Hatter joined in.

'Why is a raven like a writing-desk?' he asked Alice.

'I believe I can guess that...' began Alice.

'Do you mean you think you can find out the answer?' said the March Hare.

'Exactly so,' said Alice.

'Then you should say what you mean,' the March Hare went on.

'I do,' Alice answered. 'At least, I mean what I say and that's the same thing, you know!'

'Not the same thing at all!' said the Hatter. 'You might as well say that *"I see what I eat"* is the same thing as *"I eat what I see"*!'

'You might as well say,' added the March Hare, 'that *"I like what I get"* is the same thing as *"I get what I like"*!'

Alice did not quite know what to say to this. Then the Mad Hatter took out his watch and looked at it. He shook it every now and then and held it to his ear.

'Two days wrong!' he said. 'I told you butter wouldn't suit the works.' He looked angrily at the March Hare.

'It was the *best* butter!' said the March Hare.

'Yes, but some crumbs must have got in as well,' the Hatter grumbled. 'You shouldn't have put it in with the bread knife!'

The March Hare took the watch and looked at it gloomily. Then he dipped it in his cup of tea and looked at it again. 'Let's change the subject,' he said. 'I vote the young lady tells us a story.'

'I don't know one!' said Alice in alarm.

'Then the Dormouse shall!' they both cried. 'Wake up, Dormouse!' They pinched it on both sides at once, and the Hatter poured a little hot tea on its nose.

'I wasn't asleep!' murmured the Dormouse. 'I heard every word you said!'

'Tell us a story!' said the March Hare.

'Yes, please do,' said Alice.

The Dormouse's story

The Dormouse's story was about three little sisters.

'Their names were Elsie, Lacie and Tillie. They lived at the bottom of a well.'

'What did they live on?' asked Alice, curiously.

'They lived on treacle,' said the Dormouse.

'They couldn't have,' said Alice. 'They'd have been ill!'

'So they were,' said the Dormouse. 'Very ill.'

'Have some more tea!' said the Mad Hatter to Alice.

'I haven't had any yet, so how can I have any more?'

'You mean you can't have *less*!' said the Hatter. 'It's easy to have *more* than nothing!'

Alice turned to the Dormouse. 'Why did they live at the bottom of a well?' she asked.

'It was a treacle well,' said the Dormouse. 'These sisters were learning to draw, you see.'

'What did they draw?' asked Alice.

'Treacle,' said the Dormouse.

'I don't understand,' said Alice. 'Where did they draw the treacle from?'

'You can draw water from a water well,' said the Hatter, 'so why shouldn't you draw treacle from a treacle well?'

'But they were *in* the well!' cried Alice.

'Of course they were,' said the Dormouse. '*Well* in!' He was getting sleepy again.

'They drew everything that begins with an **M**,' he went on drowsily, 'such as Mousetraps and the Moon and Muchness. You say ''Things are much of a Muchness'' – did you ever see a drawing of a Muchness?'

'I don't *think* – ' began Alice.

'Then you shouldn't *talk*!' snapped the Hatter.

This was too much for Alice! She got up and walked into the wood. When she looked back, she saw that the others were trying to put the Dormouse into the teapot.

The Queen's croquet ground

Alice noticed a tree trunk in front of her, with a door in it. She opened it and found herself back in the hall with the glass table and the gold key.

'This time I know what to do!' she said, and she nibbled some of the mushroom till she was small enough to go through the little door into the lovely garden with its flowerbeds and fountains.

Alice was surprised to see three gardeners busily painting a white rose tree red, and even more when she saw that they were playing-cards. They were oblong and flat, with hands and feet at the corners. Their names were Two, Five and Seven.

'You see, Miss, this here rose tree ought to have been red,' Two was explaining. 'If the Queen sees it, we shall all have our heads chopped off.'

'Hush!' whispered Five.
'Here she comes!' and all
three fell flat on their faces.

Alice looked round. First came
ten soldiers, carrying clubs. Then
came ten courtiers, decorated with
diamonds. Then ten little royal children,
with hearts on their tunics.

Next came the guests, including the Duchess and the White Rabbit. And then came the Knave of Hearts, carrying a crown on a red velvet cushion. Last of all in the grand procession came the King and Queen of Hearts themselves.

Alice curtsied to the Queen and told her her name. 'I needn't be afraid of them!' she thought. 'They're only a pack of cards!'

The Queen looked at the gardeners lying flat. 'Turn them over!' she said to the knave. The gardeners jumped up and started bowing to everybody.

'Off with their heads!' cried the Queen, and the procession moved off.

'You shan't be beheaded!' said Alice and she popped the gardeners into a large flower pot, before the soldiers could catch them.

The game of croquet

Alice ran and caught up with the procession.
'Get to your places!' shouted the Queen in a
voice like thunder.

It was the strangest game of croquet Alice

had ever seen.

The balls were curled-up
hedgehogs. The mallets were flamingoes. The
soldiers had to double up and stand on their
hands to make the arches. By the time Alice had
tucked her flamingo under her arm and put its
head in position to tap the ball, her hedgehog
had uncurled and crawled away.

The players did not wait for turns and
quarrelled over their hedgehogs. The Queen
stamped about, shouting, 'Off with his (or her)
head!' every few minutes.

Soon the game was over. All the players,
except the King and Queen and Alice, had been
sentenced to be beheaded. Alice was relieved to
hear the King whisper to them, 'You are all
pardoned.'

Alice was talking to the Duchess, when a
trumpet sounded in the distance.

'The trial's beginning! Come on!' said the Duchess, taking Alice by the hand.

'What trial is that?' Alice panted as she ran after her.

Who stole the tarts?

The courtroom was crowded with small birds and animals, as well as the whole pack of cards. The King and Queen of Hearts were sitting on their thrones. The King was Judge. He wore a wig, with his crown on top of it.

Near him stood the White Rabbit, with a trumpet in one hand and a scroll of parchment in the other. The Knave of Hearts was standing in chains, between two soldiers.

On a table was a dish of tarts. (Alice hoped that they were the refreshments.)

There was a jury box with twelve creatures in it: animals, birds and a small lizard named Bill. They were all writing on slates. 'They're putting down their names, in case they forget them,' whispered the Duchess, digging her sharp little chin into Alice's shoulder.

'Stupid things!' said Alice in a loud voice.

'SILENCE IN COURT!' cried the White Rabbit. The jury were busy writing down 'Stupid things!'

Bill the Lizard's pencil squeaked. Alice could not stand that, so she went round behind him and quietly took it away. The poor little juror searched for it, and then tried to write on his slate with his finger. But, of course, it made no mark.

'Herald! Read the accusation!' said the King, sternly.

The White Rabbit blew three blasts on his trumpet, unrolled his scroll, and read:

'The Queen of Hearts she made some tarts,
 All on a summer's day.
The Knave of Hearts, he stole those tarts,
 And took them clean away.'

'Consider your verdict!' cried the King.

'Not yet, your Majesty!' the Rabbit hastily interrupted. 'The trial comes first!'

'Call the first witness!' said the King.

The evidence

This was the Mad Hatter. He had a teacup in one hand, and a piece of bread and butter in the other.

'You ought to have finished your tea by now,' said the King. 'When did you begin?'

'Fourteenth of March, I think,' said the Hatter.

'Fifteenth,' said the March Hare, who was also in the courtroom.

'Sixteenth,' said the Dormouse, who was sitting next to Alice.

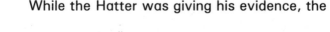

'Write that down,' said the King. The jury eagerly wrote it down and added it up.

'Give your evidence and don't be nervous,' said the King, 'or I'll have you executed on the spot!'

While the Hatter was giving his evidence, the

Dormouse complained to Alice, 'I wish you wouldn't squeeze me so!'

'I can't help it,' said Alice. 'I'm growing!'

'Then grow somewhere else. You've no right to grow here!' grumbled the Dormouse.

'Call the next witness!' said the King.

The White Rabbit, in his shrill little voice, read out the name 'ALICE!'

Alice's evidence

'Here!' cried Alice and jumped up, forgetting how large she had grown. She knocked over the jury box and the jurors went sprawling into the crowd. Alice picked them up and stuffed them

into the box.

'We cannot proceed till *all* the jury are in their proper places!' said the King, severely.

Alice saw that Bill the Lizard was upside down, so she put him back the right way up.

'What do you know about this business?' asked the King.

'Nothing!' said Alice.

'That's very important!' said the King.

'*Un*important, your Majesty means,' said the White Rabbit, anxiously. Some of the jury wrote down 'Important', some wrote 'Unimportant' and some wrote both.

Then the King read out, '*Rule forty-two* – all persons more than a mile high to leave the court.' Everyone looked at Alice.

'That's not a regular rule! You've just invented it!' said Alice.

'It's the oldest rule in the book!'

'Then it ought to be *Number one*!' said Alice.

'Consider your verdict!' said the King.

'No!' said the Queen. 'Sentence first, verdict after!'

'Stuff and nonsense!' cried Alice, loudly. 'The *idea* of having the sentence first!'

'Hold your tongue!' said the Queen, turning purple.

'I won't!' said Alice.

'OFF WITH HER HEAD!' the Queen shouted, at the top of her voice.

'Who cares for you?' said Alice. (She had grown to her full size by this time.) 'You're nothing but a pack of cards!'

At this, the whole pack rose up in the air and came flying down on her.

Alice wakes up

Alice gave a little scream, half of fright and half of anger, and tried to beat them off.

She found herself lying on the grassy bank, with her head in her sister's lap. Her sister gently brushed away some of the dead leaves that had fluttered down from the tree upon Alice's face.

'Wake up, Alice dear!' she said. 'What a long sleep you've had!'